Ready to Read?

Yup!

Bing

YUK!

by
Ted Dewan

HarperCollins *Children's Books*

Round the corner,
Not far away,
Bing's been chewing toys all day.

Hello Bing.

Hello Flop.

Maybe it's time for a snack.

Wash hands. Dry hands.

How would you
like to try
Flop's favourite food?

It's a
yummy

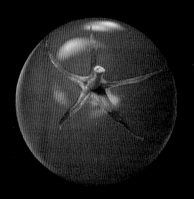

tomato

YUK! YUKKY TOMATO!

Why yuk, Bing?

You like

juicy kiwi

and
you
like

gooey
cheese.

You
like

sweet apple

and bright red strawberries.

so you will love...

a sweet and gooey
and red and juicy

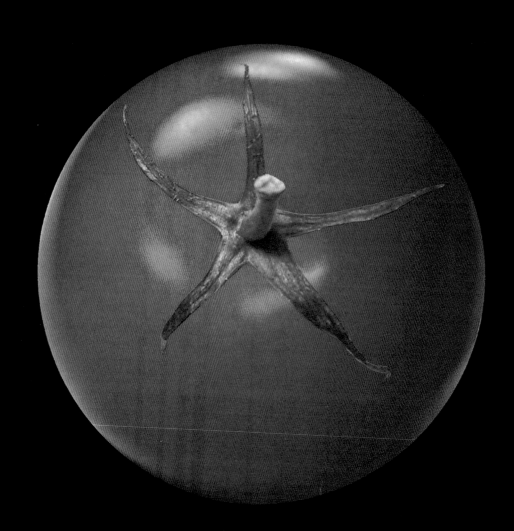

tomato

You like  snappy
carrot

and roundy egg.

You like **tasty** **orange**

and **fun** **banana.**

So...
wouldn't you **really**
like something

sweet

juicy

red

gooey

snappy

roundy

tasty

fun

Wouldn't you love to try a yummy...

tomato

That was very
naughty, Bing.

Better
have some
'time out'.

Bing,
it's OK
if you don't
like tomatoes.

How about
a snappy
carrot instead?

YUP!

Tomatoes.
They're just nOt
a Bing Thing!

juicy kiwi

gooey cheese

fun banana

stuffed sandwich

What do YOU like to eat?

tasty orange

bright red strawberries

fishy finger

slippy sushi

snappy carrot

jolly biscuits

like

! tomato !

yuk

chewy bagel

rolly peas

roundy egg

squish tomato

sweet apple

licky ice cream

crunchy broccoli

Bing again? Yup!

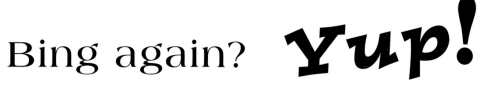

978-0-00-751477-9

978-0-00-751479-3

978-0-00-751540-0

978-0-00-751542-4

by
Ted Dewan

First published in hardback in Great Britain by David Fickling Books in 2004. This edition published in paperback by HarperCollins Children's Books in 2014.   3 5 7 9 10 8 6 4 2   ISBN: 978-0-00-751544-8
HarperCollins Children's Books is a division of HarperCollins Publishers Ltd. Text and illustrations copyright © Ted Dewan 2004, 2014. The author/illustrator asserts the moral right to be identified as the author/illustrator of the work.
A CIP catalogue record for this title is available from the British Library. All rights reserved. No part of this publication may be reproduced, stored in a retrieval system, or transmitted in any form or by any means electronic, mechanical,
photocopying, recording or otherwise, without the prior permission of HarperCollins Publishers Ltd, 1 London Bridge Street, London SE1 9GF. Visit our website at: www.harpercollins.co.uk. Printed and bound in China